First published 1990 by L'École des Loisirs, 11 Rue de Sèvres 75006 Paris, France.
First published in the U.S. by Hyperion Books for Children, 114 Fifth Avenue,
New York, New York 10011.
FIRST EDITION
1 3 5 7 9 10 8 6 4 2

Library of Congress Cataloging-in-Publication Data

Krings, Antoon. Oliver's bicycle/Antoon Krings—1st ed. p. cm. Summary: Oliver gets in trouble when he rides his bicycle inside the house on a rainy day. ISBN 1-56282-164-4 (trade)—ISBN 1-56282-165-2 (lib. bdg.) [1. Bicycles and bicycling—Fiction.] I. Title. PZ7.K8965No 1992 [E]—dc20 91-25030 CIP AC

Oliver's Bicycle

Antoon Krings

Hyperion Books for Children

Today Oliver wants to ride his bicycle.

But it's raining.

He can't go outside.

Oliver is bored.

He turns on the TV.

A bear is doing handstands

on a bicycle.

"Look, Valentine,

I can do tricks, too."

Valentine thinks

this one is too easy.

"Watch!" says Oliver.

"This one's even harder!"

Now Oliver is going to try

riding down the stairs.

Oh, no!

The bicycle twists around sharply

and throws Oliver into the air.

Oliver starts to cry.

"My bicycle is broken!"

While the bicycle is being fixed,

Valentine takes Oliver

to the merry-go-round.

On a handsome motorcycle,

Oliver is happy again.